Ike and Mama and the Block Wedding

Ike and Mama and the Block Wedding

by Carol Snyder
drawings by Charles Robinson

Coward, McCann and Geoghegan, Inc.
New York

To my parents with love;
and to the South Bronx, whose
cooperative spirit—unlike its buildings—
will not be destroyed.

Library of Congress Cataloging in Publication Data

Snyder, Carol. Ike and Mama and the block wedding.

SUMMARY: Rosie Weinstein is getting mar-
ried on Sunday but not without a little help from
the residents of East 136th Street.
[1. Weddings—Fiction. 2. Neighborliness—
Fiction. 3. Jews in the United States—Fiction. 4.
New York (City)— Fiction] I. Robinson, Charles.
II. Title.
PZ7.S68517Ih   [Fic]   78-11702
ISBN 0-698-20461-1

Printed in the United States of America

Contents

1. Mama in a Hurry

"Mama!" Ike called as he dashed in, sliding on the kitchen floor.

"Ikey dear, the house is on fire the way you're shouting?" Mama stopped stirring the clothes in the gigantic washing pot that bubbled on the black coal stove. She put both hands on Ike's flushed cheeks. They were red as strawberries from the summer heat.

"Mrs. Weinstein is outside on the front stoop crying," Ike said, as much with his hands as with his mouth. "She said for me to get you."

"Oy!" Mama moaned. She didn't bother to take the wooden stirring stick from the huge pot, but left the old cut-down broomstick handle pointing out the window. "Did she break something? A bone, maybe, God forbid?" And without waiting for an answer, Mama headed out of the kitchen toward the door to the hall outside the apartment, her full black skirt swishing past Papa's soft parlor chair—the one with the rip in it—the shelf filled with little glass animals, and the crystal dish, so fine that a rabbi could eat from it.

Ike dashed behind her yelling, "Mrs. Weinstein says her heart is broken."

"A heart attack?" Mama moved faster, clutching at her own heart.

"No, Mama." Ike tried to get Mama to understand. He grabbed for her red-checked apron strings, but although Mama was only four feet seven inches and Ike, at eleven, was just as tall, she moved faster than Ike. She seemed to whirl ahead of him.

"But Mama," Ike went on anyway, "Mrs. Weinstein says she must now break her daughter Rosie's heart, too."

"What kind of craziness is this? That's *meshugge,* all this talk of broken hearts," Mama muttered, stopping at the third-floor stair landing. Her blue eyes sparkled at Ike as she turned and pointed to their apartment. "And close the door, Ikey, cats come up."

Ike knew Mama was excited—whenever she got excited she would talk faster. Ike closed the door quickly with one hand, and with the other he held Mama by the arm so she would listen to the rest of the message.

"Mrs. Weinstein is crying because her heart is broken because she has to break her daughter Rosie's heart and tell her she has no money to pay for the rented hall for Rosie's wedding on Sunday because Mr. Weinstein, Rosie's father . . ."

"Go on," Mama nudged Ike.

"Mr. Weinstein, Mrs. Weinstein's husband, Morton Weinstein's father . . ."

"Ikey, tell already, tell!" Mama raised her eyebrow and Ike quickly finished the message.

"Just like Papa—Mr. Weinstein lost his job at the factory." Ike looked into Mama's eyes. He saw the sparkle disappear as Mama sighed.

"Oy, oy, oy, 1919 is not an easy year for any of us on this block. Not when it comes to jobs. The war over there is ended, yes"—Mama pointed to wherever she thought Europe was—"but, over here, now, there are so many people coming home to not enough jobs." Mama moaned and looked up, toward the gas light. Then she pointed a pudgy finger at the light, waved her finger from side to side, and said, "But! God willing! There will be no broken hearts on East One Hundred and Thirty-sixth Street in the Bronx!"

And Ike knew that when Mama *said*, everyone listened. God, too? Ike wondered. And somehow Ike knew he and Mama might be able to solve the problem of Rosie's wedding, and he thought, If God wants to help Mama and me make a wedding, why not?

2. Worries

Ike stood behind Mama at the top of the stoop. If he stood on tiptoes he could see over Mama's head, to where his first cousins Sammy and Dave and his second cousins Bernie and Sol were playing Johnny-on-the-Pump. Each boy bent over and clutched the waist of the boy in front. They formed a chain of bodies firmly anchored to Robert, who was clinging to the fire hydrant, the pump. Tony Golida ran, shouting, "Johnny-on-the-Pump, ONE, TWO, THREE" as he leaped onto Robert's back from behind. Ike wanted to dash down the steps and join in.

But Mrs. Weinstein, sitting on the stoop, didn't seem to hear the boys. She didn't seem to hear Ike's little sister, Bessie, playing Ring around the Rosie with her friends, either. She didn't even hear the clatter of horse hooves or the fruitman calling, "Melons, all kinds melons." Mrs. Weinstein just sat on the top step and cried.

Mama turned and pointed a pudgy finger at Ike. "Now," she said, "we are not to be interrupted. When two mamas are talking, all the BUT-MAMA-THISes and the CAN-I-DO-THATs must wait. You understand, Ikey?" She gently grasped his chin with her fingers.

The way Mama was holding his chin, Ike could not say if he understood or not. He could not say anything.

"You are to disappear like pancakes from a platter," Mama added. And she let go of Ike's chin, rumpled his curly hair, and wedged herself down onto the rest of the top step beside Mrs. Weinstein.

"But Mama," Ike started to say. All he wanted was to get past the two women. If he hurried he could surely get on top of his cousin Dave. Johnny-on-the-Pump was Ike's favorite game. But he was trapped on the stoop behind two seated bottoms that left no room for him to squeeze by. Ike lifted his foot, but he couldn't find a place for it so he put it down again.

"Oy," Mama said to Mrs. Weinstein, "I heard about your troubles with the wedding."

Now Tony Golida was waving to Ike and calling, "Hey, Ikey, we need you." And James Higgins and

Morton Weinstein were coming down East 136th
Street kicking a flattened tin can. Ike had to get past.
He tried to step down on Mama's side. As Mama
offered Mrs. Weinstein a corner of her checked apron
to wipe a huge tear that trickled down Mrs. Weinstein's rosy cheek, Ike put his foot down again. Mama
turned around and gave a look. One eyebrow was
raised, and that meant "Mama trouble." Mama never
had to raise her voice, just her eyebrow.

"So," said Mama to Mrs. Weinstein, "it's no shame
to lose a job. Who knows, maybe the next job will be
better. Maybe a tailor shop yet, not a factory."

Mrs. Weinstein sniffed and started crying again as
she said, "But the wedding. Two days away! How can I
tell Rosie there will be no wedding? No job means no
money to pay for the hall we rented. No money to buy
a wedding cake with layers and candy pearls; the kind
of cake Rosie and Arnold planned and dreamed about.
No job means no money, which means no wedding,
for sure. On Sunday yet, two days away only."

Mama put her hand on Mrs. Weinstein's sleeve.
"You won't tell her," Mama said. "If we could figure
out a way to escape from Russia to America, you and I,
we can have the common sense to figure out how to
make a wedding for Rosie. Right?"

Ike was about to sneak past when Mrs. Weinstein

called, "Ike!" and reached out and grabbed the bulky bottom of his brown tweed knickers, right above the buckle. Ike clutched the iron rail to catch his balance. "Do you hear your Mama talking?" Mrs. Weinstein asked.

But she didn't let Ike answer. Still clutching his pants, Mrs. Weinstein went on, "It's easy for your Mama to say 'We'll figure out how,' but the whole block is invited, besides relatives." She let go of the material and put her hand on Mama's shoulder. Ike was beginning to feel desperate.

"This time, Eva," Mrs. Weinstein said to Mama, "you will not be able to help. Two days only, a lost cause."

Ike thought it was a lost cause to try to get by Mama and Mrs. Weinstein. He wondered how Mama would solve the wedding problem, but more, he wondered how he would solve his own getting-down-the-steps-to-play problem, until . . . he thought about jumping over Mama. He jumped up and down practicing for the leap.

Mama turned to him. "What's this, Ikey? You're a frog, maybe?" And she swatted his left leg. "When Mamas are talking, jumping is out of the question. We are not to be interrupted, remember!" Mama turned again to face Mrs. Weinstein.

Ike felt like screaming! Then he remembered the clothes still boiling on the stove upstairs. He took a breath.

"Mama," he said.

"Shush, Ikey," Mama said, waving a hand but looking at Mrs. Weinstein. "So, Minnie," Mama continued, "two heads are better than one. We will just have to make a special plan for weddings. Weddings without money."

"Mama," Ike said.

"Not now," Mama muttered.

"But Mama," he insisted. "If the house was on fire could I interrupt?"

"What kind of talk is that?" Mama asked, putting a hand on her hip and turning to see Ike. "There's no smoke," she added.

"But the clothing must be very clean by now. It's still boiling on the stove," Ike said, waving to Tony Golida that he'd be only a minute longer. "Or burning," he added for effect.

"*Oy!*" Mama leaped up. "Come upstairs," she said, giving Mrs. Weinstein's hand a yank. "Bessie, you don't go in the street, you hear?" she called to Ike's little sister. "Why didn't you tell me sooner, Ikey?" Mama asked as she walked inside the doorway.

"You said . . ." Ike began, but Mama was gone.

Finally Ike dashed down the stairs and leaped as hard as he could, landing with a thud on top of Tony's back. But as the bottom bridge of boys collapsed, Ike's pleasure at scoring points for his team was spoiled by a terrible thought about Rosie's wedding—a terrible problem with it, or rather *without* it.

"Without Rosie's wedding," Ike said to Sammy and Dave, "there will be no wedding cake or honey cake."

"Without Rosie's wedding," he said to Bernie and Sol, "there will be no herring."

"Without Rosie's wedding," he said to Danny and Tony and Patrick and all the others, "there will be no anything!"

With Ike in the lead, the fourteen boys bounded up the stairs to help Mrs. Weinstein, Mama, and, of course, God.

3. Ike and Mama in Action

Huffing and puffing from racing up three flights of stairs, one hand hanging on to his cap, Ike pushed open the unlocked door. The breeze made a lace doily fly right off the soft parlor chair with the rip. A smell of chicken soup filled the air, mingling with the leftover morning baking smell of challah bread and honey cake. Ike's mouth watered at the thought of tonight's special Sabbath meal. Chicken was a treat, too expensive to be eaten anytime but Friday at sundown.

The thirteen boys followed Ike. They crowded into the parlor after each one stopped to carefully wipe his feet on the ragged old no-color mat outside the apartment door. The boys knew they were always welcome in Ike's house, even in the parlor, as long as they wiped their feet. Mama always told Ike she'd rather his friends mess up her parlor than get into a mess in the street.

"So, the army's here already?" Mama called from the kitchen, where she and Mrs. Weinstein reached into the boiled-dry laundry pot and examined each shirt, then hung it on the fire-escape clothesline. "Close the door, Ikey, cats come up," Mama added.

Then she brought out a big round bowl of cream-colored peas covered with specks of black pepper, and put it on the little table in front of Papa's parlor chair.

"A handful of arbis never spoiled an appetite yet," she said. "So eat!" Mama waved her hands at the boys.

"Chick-peas," said Tony Golida, recognizing the small round vegetable. He popped four of the peppery balls into his mouth at one time. A startled look came over his face, and he suddenly dashed toward the kitchen for some water to put out the fire in his throat. Mama followed Tony to give him a glass.

In the parlor, the other boys sat down on the faded, threadbare, red-flowered rug. Except Danny Mantussi. He couldn't find a spot for his long legs, so he stood in his usual space admiring Mama's collection of glass animals on the shelf. Ike noticed that when Danny reached over to take a handful of arbis, his big hands got twice as many as anyone else.

Ike glanced at Mama through the kitchen doorway. Before Mama stepped back from the open kitchen window she called out to Ike's little sister.

"Bessie," she yelled, "you watch for Papa and *yoo-hoo* when you see him, and don't run in the street after your rubber-band ball. Toys we can get new ones, Bessies we can't." She turned back. "Maybe today Papa will have found work," she said to everyone and no one at the same time.

"Mama, I have brought you our fourteen more heads to help with the special plan for Rosie's wedding," Ike called.

Mama and Mrs. Weinstein and Tony Golida came into the parlor. Mama looked at Ike, who was sitting cross-legged on the flowered rug, leaned over with an *"oy,"* and poked him with her pudgy finger. "And fourteen bellies to be filled at Rosie's wedding, *nu?*" Mama smiled knowingly.

Ike and the other boys smiled. At the mention of the word "wedding," Mrs. Weinstein started to sob again. Morton Weinstein whispered to his best friend, James Higgins, "What's such a fuss about my dopey sister Rosie's wedding? Rosie and my mother will cry the whole time anyway and they wouldn't see anything. Just uninvite everybody."

"Morton." Mrs. Weinstein squinted at her son, whose whisper could always be heard in the next apartment. "Look ashamed from such talk. This is not just any wedding. Your sister Rosie is marrying a high-school graduate, a scholar perhaps, whose family lives uptown on the Grand Concourse, even. And what a Rosie, a salesgirl, all day on her feet and never complains. Never asks for anything. So why shouldn't such a girl have her dream come true?" And she started to cry again. "Oy," she sobbed to Mama. "And the wedding dress you made, I cannot even pay for. This time, Eva, it is a lost cause. This is a problem on East One Hundred and Thirty-sixth Street with no answer."

"Problems with no answer," Mama said, "sometimes take a little longer. So we will sit here and wait for the answer." Mama pulled in a kitchen chair and sat down, her black skirt plumped like an umbrella around her. For a long time she didn't make a sound. The boys didn't make a sound either. Only Mrs. Weinstein's sobs could be heard. Once Mama stood up and said, "Maybe." Then she waved her hand as if pushing the idea away, and sat down again.

"I have an idea," said Sammy.

"What is it, Sammy darling? Speak up," Mama said.

"Tell Rosie's boyfriend's Mama to make the wedding," he said, and sat down waiting to see Mama's reaction.

Mrs. Weinstein sobbed the biggest sob yet.

"It is good that you are using your brain," said Mama, "but that idea is out of the question. The *bride's* Mama and Papa must make the wedding. That's the way it's done."

"I have an idea," said Danny.

"What?" asked Mama.

"Let's have another handful of chick-peas to help us think."

Mama nodded to the bowl.

The silence seemed to grow heavier and heavier. Suddenly, Ike, feeling he must say something, jumped up with excitement to say, "Well, at least we have fourteen heads to help!" Only his big foot got caught on Danny Mantussi's even bigger foot. Ike grabbed the nearby shelf for balance. There was a crash, the sound of breaking glass, and Mama's favorite glass animal, an elephant, lay on the floor, missing a trunk and one leg. Ike wished he could vanish like a chip of ice on a hot day.

All the boys gasped, waiting for "Mama trouble."

"You see?" said Mrs. Weinstein. "An omen, bad luck for certain."

Ike felt like the biggest klutz on East 136th Street in the Bronx. Although it was only a second before Mama spoke, it seemed like an hour to Ike. He looked up at her. But her eyes didn't sparkle. There was no

"Mama trouble." She reached out her soft arms to Ike, hugged him, and said with a glance to Mrs. Weinstein, "No; it's a *mazel tov,* Ikey, *good* luck!"

Ike looked up in amazement. He opened his eyes wide. "But Mama," he said, "why is breaking your favorite glass elephant good luck?"

Mama crossed her arms and pointed her tiny nose to the gas light. "It's a *mazel tov,*" she said, "because: What good luck it wasn't my special glass plate that broke—the plate a rabbi could eat from, proudly!"

Ike wanted to make Mama laugh, just to know she really wasn't sad about the glass animal. "Eleven-year-old boys have big feet," Ike said. "I brought you fourteen heads to help, but I also brought you twenty-eight big feet."

Mama did laugh and she rumpled Ike's hair. Ike felt better and he watched Danny Mantussi take a big handful of chick-peas. Everyone was quiet again as Mama thought some more. Only Danny's munching sounds broke the silence. Ike wanted Mama to laugh again, so he added, "And I brought you twenty-eight big hands."

But this time Mama didn't laugh. She didn't even chuckle. Ike got worried again. Now what had he done? Everyone was silently watching Mama. Waiting for her to say or do something. First Mama started to nod her head. Then she jumped up and said, "Hands!"

Finally Mama grabbed Ikey and said, "Oy, Ikey, are you smart!" And she pinched his cheek until it was red.

The boys looked at each other. Then they looked at Ike.

Ike knew he'd done something terrific. Ike knew he must have said something brilliant. But he wasn't sure what it was. He just knew it must have something to do with hands.

"Of course, hands," said Mama. "You see, you wait long enough, the answer comes. So we have now twenty-eight hands plus four from you and me," she added to Mrs. Weinstein, "and I know from where we can get some more. So a decision is reached."

Ike scratched his curly head. What decision? he wondered.

"With a thank-you to Ikey and his cousins and friends, we now have a special plan for weddings," Mama said, and she nodded.

"Whatever it is, it won't work," muttered Mrs. Weinstein.

Ike and his friends and cousins looked at each other.

"What did we do?" whispered Patrick to Robert.

"I don't know," answered Ike's second cousins Bernie and Sol.

Ike, too, shrugged his shoulders and offered everyone another handful of arbis to celebrate the special plan they'd made but only Mama knew. What could it be? Ike wondered as he chewed.

"Hands that can scoop up," Mama muttered.

4. A Special Plan for Weddings

Ike and his friends stopped chewing chick-peas and froze in their places on the faded rug when Mama pointed a pudgy finger and said, "No one is to move. We have under two hours till sundown, and a day's work to do. Tomorrow on the Sabbath we only think about, we do not do."

"And you'll never do it," cried Mrs. Weinstein. "*Impossible* with no money!" And another flood of tears started.

Mama put her hands on her hips, turned her head to the side, and said, "Minnie Weinstein, enough already. Tears are to wash away problems so your eyes can see what to do next. Tears are not to drown in. So." Mama stopped and looked into Mrs. Weinstein's eyes. "They are clear enough, your eyes. Go get the wedding dress from on my bed."

Even Mrs. Weinstein listened to Mama. She scurried into the back room.

"Bernie! Sol! Ikey! Dave! Sammy! Morton!" Mama stepped over bodies in the crowded parlor and tapped heads as she called names. "We start the special plan."

The boys all looked at each other and some of them shrugged their shoulders. Patrick scratched his head. All were wondering what the special plan was. But Mama didn't seem to notice. She pointed to the kitchen. "Two boys will go drag out the ice pan from under the icebox. They will empty it and dry it well and take it door to door for flour." Mama's long skirt swirled as she turned and pointed to the hall. "Two more boys are to borrow another icebox pan, wash and dry it, and fill it door to door with sugar. No one on East One Hundred and Thirty-sixth Street can afford to donate a wedding cake—a wedding cake fit for a bride with a groom, a high-school graduate. But!"—and Mama folded her arms, crushing her white puffy sleeves—"each family can certainly give a handful of flour—and a handful of sugar." Mama nodded with each ingredient she mentioned: "A shmear of butter and a cup of milk." Then Mama unfolded her arms and pointed to the boys once again.

"So two more boys with pots to put milk and butter in and one more boy will walk with the others to ask

30

for and scoop up handfuls. Ike, you will please choose who is who. So! We will now put into action the 'handful plan' for weddings. I will take care of getting the hands to help with the salads and herring, and when Papa comes home we will have him take care of the wine."

Mama seemed to have a list in her head, and with a nod she put a check next to each problem solved. But Ike now had a new problem. Carrying all that sugar and flour on this hot day would not be a good job. Carrying a pot of milk or a pot of butter was not fun, either. Full pans were heavy and there were a lot of stairs to walk up and down.

But the job of scooper would be fun. It would be like being a boss. The scooper would be in charge. Better yet, the scooper could lick sugar from his fingers. The scooper could enjoy the feel of the powdery flour. Ike knew he could not take the good job for himself, for sure, yet he yearned for it. All the boys were raising their hands, waving like in school, and saying, "I'll scoop, I'll scoop." Ike didn't know what to do.

Mama didn't notice. "So," she said, "with the what-to-eat solved, the army is to return before two hours and then meet here again tomorrow night at sundown for baking and decorating a wedding cake with candy pearls and butter-cream icing . . . with

31

flowers even!" And Mama shrugged her shoulders. "A good thing I already finished making the wedding dress," she said, watching Mrs. Weinstein carry it over her arm as she came from the bedroom. Then Mrs. Weinstein started to cry again.

"Don't drip on satin," Mama yelled, so loudly that Ike jumped.

"I can't take a wedding dress I can't pay for. No job—no money—no wedding dress." Mrs. Weinstein handed the dress back to Mama. "What will you live on next week if I can't pay?" Mrs. Weinstein said. "How will you pay for food?"

Ike, happy for a moment not to think about whom to choose for scooper, ran to the little tea can nailed to a shelf in the kitchen. He didn't even stop to rub his knee when he banged himself on the cement sink as he jumped up and reached inside the tin. "The 'handful plan' again," said Ike, "but instead of flour, a handful of pennies from each family." Ike finished his sentence, took out some pennies from the tin *pushka*, and put them in Mrs. Weinstein's hand.

"Charity I should take?" Mrs. Weinstein cried harder. "Shoes off the children's feet, maybe? And Ike," she said, "your brain is as curly as your hair. You give me your mama's pennies to pay your mama for weeks of sewing this most beautiful dress! *Meshugge!*"

Mama cleared her throat, squinted her eyes, and patted Ike on the head. Then she said to Mrs. Weinstein, "Your Morton's brain should be as curly." Mama sighed. "Not charity," she said, and she put her hands on her hips. "My Ikey has come up with an idea for . . . a business investment."

Ike knew that those were very important words.

"A *what?*" said Mrs. Weinstein.

"A business investment," Mama repeated. "One day my Bessie may need a wedding dress. One day Mrs. Golida's Maria may need a wedding dress. One day Mrs. Mantussi's Paulina may need a wedding dress, too."

"So?" said Mrs. Weinstein.

"So?" said the boys.

"So?" said Mama. "With a little lace added here and a pearl or a flower changed there we could have a different wedding dress for all the different weddings. Just like the people on this block," Mama added, "a lot the same, a little bit different, and each one special!" Mama folded her arms triumphantly. "So!" she said. "If everyone wants to invest ten pennies for their daughter's future? That's charity?" Mama nodded, making another check on the list in her head.

And to Ike, she said, "So the scooper will also have pockets, to be filled with pennies, door to door. So choose already, Ikey." Mama waved at him as if chasing pigeons.

That brought Ike back to his own problem. Whom to choose for the job of scooper and penny collector, a job of importance. Hands waved at Ike.

"Me, Ike, me," shouted Bernie, waving both hands.

"He's too strong," said Tony. "He should help carry."

"You're strong too, Tony," said Ike, pointing to the icebox pan, "so you help Bernie carry the pan of flour."

"So me." Patrick waved. "I'd be a good scooper. What about me?"

Ike looked around. He considered telling Patrick he wanted the job of scooper for himself, but that sounded babyish. Then he remembered what Mama had said. The scooper must have pockets to fill with pennies. "No pockets," he said, looking at Patrick's pants.

"Okay, I'll carry the sugar with Robert," said Patrick, as if he had just done a great big favor.

"So," said Ike, pointing at his first cousins Davie and Sammy, "you knock on doors and open them."

"Okay," said Sammy and Dave, without time to think as Mrs. Weinstein barreled past, stopping only to poke shoulders. "Morton, James, and Herbie Friedman," she said, "you will take the wedding dress and bridal veil upstairs." Mrs. Weinstein did not believe in asking. She just poked and pushed and muttered. "In these apartments just our family makes a crowd."

That left Ike, Danny, Joey, Jack, and Sol as possible scoopers. Ike looked at the boys crowded together on the faded red rug. Ike listened to Danny, who was cracking the knuckles of his big hands.

"I'll do the butter," Sol volunteered. "It's better than carrying milk," he added.

"What's so bad about carrying milk?" asked Joey. "I'll carry it with Jack."

So, thought Ike, now that left just Danny and himself as possible scoopers. "He's going to choose himself for the good jobs," said Herbie, pointing to Ike.

Ike wanted to choose himself. He loved being in charge. Ike fiddled with the broken elephant while he watched Danny take another big, sweeping handful of chick-peas. Danny's huge hands must hold twice as many peas as his or any of the other boy's hands. In fact, as Ike stared at them he realized Danny's hands were as big as Papa's even, and that was big! The decision was making itself.

"So," said Ike, "the scooper will be Danny Mantussi."

"How come he gets the best job?" asked Jack.

And then Ike made all the boys happy with his answer.

"Because," he said, "if tall Danny Mantussi scoops with his big hands, there will be more flour and sugar and that means a bigger cake to eat."

"So what will you do, Ike?" Danny asked, sticking his hands in his pockets.

Ike looked at Danny's fingertips sticking through the ripped material and knew. "I will collect the pennies," Ike said. "It was my idea and my pockets have no holes." He put his hands in his pockets and smiled. Ike was happy with a job of importance.

Now the boys were all standing in the parlor. They heard Bessie *yoo-hoo*, then soon Papa opened the door. He was carrying Bessie on his shoulders.

"What's this?" bellowed Papa, putting Bessie down and huffing to catch his breath. "A hotel?"

Then he saw the wedding dress. "A wedding? There is no air in here from all these people. Crowds like this should be outside where you can breathe."

"What a good idea, Papa!" said Mama, and she reached high above her head to pat six-foot-tall Papa on his shoulder. Papa wrinkled his forehead and looked puzzled. "Like when the boy on the next block came back from the war," Mama said. "A block party they made on the street."

Ike caught on first. "A wedding outside! With banners and streamers."

"With tables of food," said Ike's first cousin Sammy.

"With a big cake that looks like a flag?" asked Bessie. "Like the boy that came home from the war had?" she added.

"A cake, yes, Bessie. A flag, no." Mama nodded, making another check in her head. "So that's that!" she said. "We will have a block wedding for Rosie and Arnold, on the street, in the fresh air. And Papa, you will please take care of the wine—a bottle of leftover Passover wine, from whomsoever. And Papa, this block wedding is a secret, a surprise." Mama seemed to look at each boy as well as Papa when she said this. "Rosie and Arnold are not to know there have been any problems with their wedding. A bride and groom should dream not worry. You hear, Bessie? Ikey? A secret wedding plan. Morton, take the dress upstairs now, and tell your mother about the secret plan. James and Herbie, help him. So go, everyone! Go!"

Mama looked out the window at the sun. "We have only a little over an hour left today before sundown; before our Sabbath begins."

The boys started out ahead of Ike.

"And close the door, Ikey," Mama yelled. "Cats come up!"

"Rosie's wedding in the street?" Papa said. "What would God think?"

"With the stars as a chuppah it has to be a blessing," said Mama.

Tony, not yet out the door, stopped.

"A chuppah is a wedding canopy," Ike explained.

And God would have the best seat, he thought as he reached for the doorknob. Then he realized how God could help.

"But Mama," Ike said. "What if it rains?"

5. The Big Mix-Up

The boys raced upstairs and down knocking on doors, collecting handfuls of flour and sugar and a pocketful of pennies, and answering a hundred questions. Patrick and Robert almost dropped the pan of sugar when a bee started after them. Tony was covered with a dusting of powdery flour. Danny Mantussi licked sugar off his fingers and Ike jingled the pennies in his pocket and said "please" and "thank you" to each neighbor.

An hour later, the army returned to Ike's apartment. They set down their pans of handfuls in the corner of the kitchen. Through the window came calls of "James, dinner's ready," "Danny, you get home this minute," and "Davie, Sammy, come quick, it is almost sundown, time to light the Sabbath candles." The boys scattered.

Mama leaned out the kitchen window and called to

the neighbors. "Tonight and tomorrow Minnie Weinstein and I can only *think* about the wedding; but we can *do* nothing on Saturday, the Jewish Sabbath, our blessed day of rest."

"So," hollered Mrs. Mantussi from downstairs, "we cannot help Sunday morning, our Christian Sabbath; we will be at church. But tonight and tomorrow we can *do* while you *think.*"

"So," said Mama, "you could, maybe, buy the herring tomorrow?"

"Of course," said Mrs. Mantussi.

"What should *we* do?" called Mrs. Golida. Her family were churchgoers, too. "Make lasagna like at our weddings?"

"Or corned beef and cabbage like at our weddings?" called Mrs. Murphy all the way from across the street.

"Not kosher," said Mama, "because your dishes and pots have been used for meat and milk together. But you could make hard-boiled eggs in the shell yet; Saturday night, after sundown, when the Sabbath is over, my sister Sadie can make it into egg salad."

"And me?" called Mrs. Higgins from upstairs. "Maybe sweet-potato pie like at our weddings?"

"You could make boiled potatoes in the skins yet," said Mama. "That would be kosher. Then Saturday night I will make a big potatonik. That is like a pancake. So," said Mama, waving her hand, "everyone on East One Hundred and Thirty-sixth Street in the Bronx will have a something to eat at Rosie's wedding."

Papa returned, his arms filled with leftover Passover wine from Aunt Sadie and Uncle Charlie and more from Aunt Ida and Uncle Abe. Mama called, "Good Sabbath," and pulled her head back inside the apartment. After the family washed their hands and faces, Papa and Ike put yarmulkes on their heads. They patted the satin skullcaps into place. Then they sat at the dining table in the parlor. On the Sabbath, like company, they used a special lace tablecloth and the good dishes. The sun went down, and Mama covered her head with a white lace kerchief, said the blessing, and lit the candles, then waved her hands gently above them. Papa, thanking God for the gift of a day of rest in their weary lives, blessed the wine and the challah bread. Mama served the chicken soup with matzo balls, and Bessie chased the plump knadlech around her bowl with a spoon. Only one challah was eaten that night. The other loaf Mama saved for the wedding.

All Friday night they prayed, thought, and rested.

All day Saturday they prayed, thought, admired the world, and rested. Then Saturday night at sundown, with the Sabbath over and with less than one day until the wedding, they sprang into action. Just after Mama had put Bessie to bed, the army of boys arrived to deliver boiled eggs, boiled potatoes, and herring.

Mama shouted orders as she began to make the wedding cake. "Papa, light the stove please." She waved her hand at him. "Bessie, get back into bed. Boys, wash your hands at the sink—with soap. Ikey," Mama said, pushing a huge bowl across the kitchen table toward him, "finish drying, then add seventeen handfuls of sugar."

Ike hung the dish towel on the wooden rod near the sink, scooped up handfuls of sugar from the icebox pan in the corner of the kitchen, and dumped each handful into the big bowl, counting, "One, two, three . . . eleven, twelve." Or was it ten, eleven?

"So quick, Ikey, pour the sugar and pass the bowl to Patrick. Patrick and Robert, add twenty-five handfuls of flour, please. Danny, for this your hands are too big, so you will stir with the wooden spoon." Mama pushed a strand of dark hair out of her sparkling blue eyes and handed Danny a spoon from the hook on the wall.

"Bessie, get back into bed," Mama scolded. "Tomorrow I will have a special something for you to do. Tonight you might get in the way. A burnt Bessie we don't need! So stir, *kinder,* stir!" She said to the boys, "Now, scoop the potatoes, Ikey, and mash them good. As soon as she can get away, Mrs. Weinstein will be here to help make the potatonik. Sammy and Davie, chop up the eggs and bring them to your mother to make into egg salad.

"*Oy,*" said Mama, as she added a pinch of this and a shake of that, shmears of butter and cups of milk, to the cake batter. The boys lined up and each one stirred till his arm ached. Danny Mantussi, Ike, Sammy, and Dave each stuck a finger into the batter when Mama wasn't looking and licked off the creamy mixture. Then Mama poured the batter into three cake pans and put the pans in the oven of the big black coal stove. Mama stopped to wipe her forehead with a corner of her checked apron.

"Now, if everyone listened and obeyed . . . the cake will be perfect. We must wait and pray," said Mama, "pray the cake doesn't fall in the middle. That is the only problem left. You must not stamp or make a noise, for sure. So take off your shoes and tiptoe. Better yet, go to the roof, children, and cool off while the cake bakes."

Mama waved her checked apron at the boys, and carrying their shoes, the boys tiptoed out the door and started up the stairs to the roof for a breath of air and maybe a breeze. Morton Weinstein poked Ike as they reached the fifth-floor landing.

"Rosie and Arnold are probably on the roof smooching. Pass it on."

Ike whispered the message to Sammy and Sammy whispered to Dave and the voices stopped completely after Morton said the usual:

"Let's go watch!"

The boys climbed the stairs, passed the fifth-floor landing, then crawled out onto the roof and hid behind the rough brick chimney. At the end of the roof, but still close enough for them to see and hear, sat Rosie and Arnold. But tonight, although they sat very close together, and although Arnold's arm was around Rosie's shoulder, they were not kissing. Tonight they were discussing.

Rosie snuggled up even closer to Arnold. Then Arnold twisted one of Rosie's side curls around his finger. Rosie looked into Arnold's eyes. "It's so good to be alone," she said.

The boys huddled behind the brick chimney, winked and smiled at each other, and watched some more. Danny Mantussi almost sneezed, but he stopped himself. And James Higgins had to clamp his hand over his mouth so he wouldn't laugh.

"We have so much to discuss," Rosie said.

Ike frowned and whispered to Morton, "Discuss? Why don't they just kiss, like usual?"

Rosie snuggled even closer to Arnold and smoothed the newspapers they sat on. "I overheard my Mama and Papa," she said, "when I went back inside to get the newspaper. They whisper like Morton. You can hear them on the next block."

"What did you hear?" Arnold asked.

"Papa is out of work." Rosie sighed. "They can't afford a wedding hall, a big cake, and all that food. Only they don't want to spoil my dream wedding. But Arnold, I don't want them to spend all that money on us."

Arnold bent down and adjusted his glasses. "Rosie," he said, "remember last week at the matinee we saw the movie where Mary Pickford eloped with Douglas Fairbanks? . . . They ran off and got married. You think maybe *we* could run off and get married?"

Rosie stared into Arnold's eyes. "A wedding would be wonderful," she said. "But Arnold, you're my dream come true; not the wedding. You're the one I love."

"Now they're gonna kiss," whispered Danny Mantussi, peeking over the chimney top.

"This is more like it," Dave muttered. "All this mushy stuff."

"Love and dream come true." Sammy hugged himself and fluttered his eyelashes like Rosie did.

The boys almost burst out laughing.

"What was that?" Rosie said.

Arnold looked around in the darkness. "Nothing," he said, and he snuggled closer. "I love you Rosie," he sighed. "I want to be with you, forever. I'd marry you anytime, anywhere."

Ike felt like yelling out—so how about a block wedding . . . outside. But it was a secret. Mama *SAID!* Oh, poor Mama, poor Mrs. Weinstein. If there was no wedding . . . poor everybody!

Rosie started to pucker her lips. So kiss already, Ike thought. We have to go downstairs.

Ike poked Morton and like a silent movie star clutched his heart and mouthed the words "No wedding."

But Morton was more interested in not missing the kiss.

Rosie was ready . . . eyes closed, lips puckered, but Arnold was still talking.

Sammy pretended to play a violin, softly humming "Hearts and Flowers" like at sad parts in the movies. But Ike didn't laugh. As Rosie and Arnold picked up the newspapers they'd put down over the tar roof and disappeared through the doorway, Ikey sat back and stared.

Then, while the other boys were jabbering about the kiss, and James Higgins, Robert Murphy, Tony Golida, and Sammy practiced kissing their own hands to make the right sound, Ike said one word: "Elope!"

"What?" James said.

"Elope!" Ike repeated. "That means run away without a wedding, without a block wedding!

"Listen!" Ike called to the boys, signaling that they should gather around him. "We can't let Rosie and Arnold elope. We've got to stop them. Otherwise all the work we did today was for NOTHING!"

"And that cake smells so good," said Danny Mantussi, sniffing the air.

The boys, too, discussed and decided. In minutes they, too, had a plan for midnight on the fire escapes of East 136th Street. A secret plan.

6. Ike and Mama Getting Ready

The boys dashed down the stairs, still carrying their shoes. The wedding plans might have collapsed but they didn't want the cake to. Ike remembered Mama's warning and tiptoed into the apartment. Tony Golida stopped to pick tar off his sock. And Danny Mantussi pulled his sock around so his big toe wouldn't stick out of the hole.

When Ike and the boys crowded into the kitchen they found that Mrs. Weinstein had joined Mama. To the mouth-watering smell of baking cake had been added the delicious smell of cooking potatonik. So much work, Ike thought. Poor Mama. Poor Mrs. Weinstein. There might be broken hearts. Ike poked Morton, reminding him not to say a word about the midnight plans. After all, Mama and Mrs. Weinstein would make a terrible noise and the cake would drop, for sure.

"You are just in time," Mama said, getting two dish towels ready to use as potholders. "So," Mama repeated the words she'd said before the boys went on the roof, "if everyone listened and obeyed . . . the cake will be perfect."

The boys all looked at each other.

"Was it seventeen handfuls of sugar and twenty-five handfuls of flour?" asked Patrick.

"Or was it seventeen handfuls of flour and twenty-five handfuls of sugar?" asked Ike, cracking his knuckles nervously.

Then the time finally came to take out the cake.

"Step back, *kinder*," Mama shouted. And using the two dish-towel potholders, she pulled out the first pan, examined it, and put it down on the table to cool.

The boys practically climbed on each other to try to see the cake. Tony Golida stood on a kitchen chair and Ike peeked right over Mama's shoulder. Danny Mantussi had no trouble seeing at all. No one said a word. They were all waiting for Mama to give a verdict. But Mama didn't say anything. She just pulled out the second cake pan. The kitchen filled with a baking smell so strong that Ike could almost see it. Ike thought he saw Mama nod as she examined the cake and put it on the table to cool. But still she said nothing. Mrs. Weinstein gently pressed the center of the cake. Mama reached into the oven and very slowly pulled out the third cake pan. The boys could almost taste the smell of the cake. Ike's stomach growled as he waited for Mama to speak. Had the boys done a good job? Would the verdict be . . . perfect?

Mama put the third cake on the table and reached into the corner of the kitchen for the broom. She turned it upside down and with a snap of the wrist pulled out a piece of straw. With the clean side down she stuck the straw into the center of the third cake. Then she quickly drew it out and felt it with her fingers.

"What's going on?" Danny Mantussi muttered.

"It's the cake test," Ike whispered, "to see if it's done."

The boys leaned closer and closer, still waiting for Mama's verdict.

Finally Mama tossed the straw aside and folded her arms. She looked at the three cakes and said the words everyone was waiting to hear.

"Perfect! A prize! And tomorrow morning when we put on icing, candy flowers, and pearls, it will be a treasure three cakes high."

"A blessing on your head," Mrs. Weinstein said to Mama, hugging her.

The boys, still afraid to make noise, shook each other's hands.

"What good boys," Mama said, patting each head.

Ike licked his lips and made believe he was reaching for the cake. Mama tapped his hand jokingly.

"I can't wait to eat it tomorrow," said James Higgins.

"Yum!" said Ike's cousin Sammy, and he made a slurping noise.

"I never saw such a big cake," said Patrick. "Not in my whole life!"

"So!" said Mama. "Now we are ready for Rosie's wedding. The cake did not drop. There will be plenty of food." And she raised her hands, tilted her head, and looked up toward the gas light which hung down from the kitchen ceiling. "Everything will be just so: a perfect wedding."

Ike cracked his knuckles nervously, but he didn't say a word about Rosie and Arnold's midnight plan. Rosie didn't want her mama to worry and Ike didn't want his mama to worry, either. When Mama couldn't see him, Ike raised an eyebrow, making sure each boy saw him and remembered the plan they too had made on the roof.

"Now go get some sleep, *kinder*. Tomorrow will be

a busy day." Mama looked around at the food. "Yes," she said, "everyone on East One Hundred and Thirty-sixth Street in the Bronx will have a something to eat at Rosie's wedding."

"And outside will be perfect, with lots of room," Mrs. Weinstein added. "So our Rosie will have her dream come true." Mama and Mrs. Weinstein hugged again.

Morton and Ike looked at each other, shook their heads, and looked back at their mamas. Ike couldn't help worrying.

The boys shouted, "So long." They put on their shoes and then clopped like horses down the stairs. Mrs. Weinstein followed them making a shushing noise that was just as loud. The clopping gave Ike an idea. "Oh, Mama," he said. "My friend the Fire Chief can help with Rosie's wedding, too."

"And what can a fire chief cook?" Mama asked.

"Not cook," said Ike. "He could block off East One Hundred and Thirty-sixth Street with horses."

"With WHAT?" shouted Mama, opening her eyes wide.

"Horses," Ike repeated.

"There will be no horses at Rosie's wedding," Mama said, "to smell up the place and bring flies.

What would the people from the Grand Concourse think? What's wrong with you, Ikey? What?"

"Not live horses, Mama." Ike laughed. "Wooden horses, like barricades, fences, to keep traffic away. Like they use at fires!"

"Oh." Mama laughed, and she pinched his cheek until it was red. "What a good idea. Oy, Ikey, it is so hot in here like a fire." Mama opened two top buttons on her blouse and fanned herself with the white cloth.

Ike knew this was the moment to start his plan. "Since it is so hot, Mama, can I take my mattress and sleep out on the fire escape tonight? Please, Mama?"

"Even on hot June nights like this, there is some-times a breeze out there. You worked hard, Ikey. You need a good night's sleep. So sleep on the fire escape if you want. But don't lean over the rails, you hear? Broken bones we don't need now when everything is perfect for Rosie's wedding."

Oy, Ike thought, not so perfect if Arnold and Rosie elope!

Like his Mama, Ike knew how to make plans. But would the plans work? Ike was worried!

7. The Secret Plan at Midnight

The fire escape was Ike's favorite place to sleep. There was always a breeze, and he loved the night sounds of window shades flapping and trains off in the distance. Ike said good night to Mama. She was shaking Papa, who was half asleep in his chair. "Wake up and go to sleep," Mama said. And she marched off with Papa shuffling behind her. Ike got into his pajama bottoms, dragged his mattress and pillow onto the moonlit fire escape, but — he didn't go to sleep.

Ike reached inside the open kitchen window and pulled the shade down. In response, shades went down on five fire escapes on East 136th Street. The secret plan had begun.

"Move over." Morton excitedly shoved Ike as he climbed down from above and sat down next to him on the bedding.

"*Sh,*" Ike said. "Mama's getting ready for bed." He

pointed to the open bedroom window. Ike wasn't taking any chances, especially with the notorious Weinstein whisper.

Ike seemed to check off a list in his mind. "You set the clock back an hour?" he whispered.

Morton nodded yes.

"You wrote the note exactly like we said on the roof? You spelled the words right?"

Morton nodded again and leaned against the rail.

"You stuck it on Rosie's windowsill with gum?"

Morton nodded yes, yes, yes, impatiently, and put his hands behind his head, elbows out.

"This plan has got to stop Arnold and Rosie," Ike whispered, reviewing the next steps. "We let Arnold get up the ladders to Rosie, find the note, and if Arnold leaves alone—good. But no way do we let him get away with Rosie. No matter what!"

Danny Mantussi coughed on the fire escape below; a signal that someone was coming. Ike's heart pounded so loud he wondered if Morton could hear it. Why was Arnold so early? Why hadn't Patrick signaled? He wasn't ready yet. A hand reached up over the rail from below. When Ike saw the hand clutching a bag, he relaxed. It was Tony Golida giving Ike the bag of water. Tony lowered himself back down next to Danny Mantussi. Now they were almost ready. All that was missing was James Higgins, and in another minute he climbed down, quietly passing Rosie's window, and down some more to Ike and Morton.

Down the moonlit block window shades were raised and lowered on Robert and Patrick's fire escape. Their signals alerted the boys that Arnold was approaching East 136th Street.

Ike practically crushed Morton's leg as he strained to see the flapping window shade on Herbie Friedman's fire escape. Someone who didn't know Ike's plan—someone like Arnold—would have thought there were a lot of restless people on East 136th Street that night. But Ike and Morton, James Higgins, Tony Golida, and Sammy and Dave knew that the signal meant Arnold was getting closer and closer.

Except for the buzz of a pesky mosquito, the whimper of a fretful baby, and Sammy and Dave on the next fire escape, pretending to snore, there wasn't a sound.

Then Ike heard Arnold's body thud against the iron ladder down below. He didn't dare look. He pictured Arnold stretching to reach the iron rung, then chinning up and climbing to the second floor, walking over the "sleeping" bodies of Danny Mantussi and Tony Golida, climbing again. Ike's heart beat faster and faster. Then Ike felt a pant leg brush by. He pretended to be sound asleep; so did Morton and James, who were huddled together next to Ike.

The boys took a breath and held it as Arnold climbed up one more ladder on the fire escape. When he reached Rosie's window Ike heard the sound of paper as Arnold read the note the boys had composed. Each of the boys knew the letter by heart.

DEAR ARNOLD,
YOU GOTTA FORGIVE ME. I CAN'T ELOP WITH YOU. MORTON HID MY SHOES.
LOVE AND KISSES
ROSIE

The boys waited for Arnold to turn around and come down the fire-escape ladder. Only he didn't.

Arnold crumpled the letter and stuck it in his pocket. Then he whispered, "Rosie. Come out. Come out."

James Higgins couldn't hold back a laugh. Ike poked him.

"Come meow-t," Sammy snickered from the next fire escape, imitating the night sounds of the cats on the street.

But when Arnold looked around, Sammy snored.

Morton smiled and puffed out his chest when Rosie whispered, "You're so early. I'm not ready. It's only eleven o'clock. And *sh,* be real quiet, Arnold. On a hot night like this people sleep on the fire escapes."

"I know, Rosie. I know." Arnold adjusted his glasses, took out his pocket watch, and lit a match. "Twelve on the dot," he said holding the watch out for Rosie to witness.

"That's strange," Rosie muttered. "Well, maybe my clock stopped. I'll be just a minute. I have to get my shoes."

Morton and Ike and James Higgins grinned in the dark, expecting Arnold to get tired of waiting for Rosie. Then maybe he'd get mad and go away. When he'd waited five minutes, Rosie said, "Where are my shoes?" But all Arnold said then was, "We've got to hurry, Rosie, before someone hears us. Forget the shoes. You can borrow shoes from my sister. I'll carry you when we get to the street."

"Oh Arnold," Rosie sighed. "This is so romantic."

Ike thought he heard Sammy make that kissing sound, like on the roof.

For the first time Ike was getting nervous. There was only one more plan, and that was supposed to be a last resort.

Arnold and Rosie climbed past Ike, hardly making a sound until Arnold said in a strained voice, "Be careful, Rosie, hold the railing."

"*Sh,*" said Rosie. "You'll wake Ike. And my brother Morton's sleeping there, too." Rosie pointed to Morton's curled-up body. Morton stretched, just to make Rosie and Arnold nervous. Rosie and Arnold continued down the next ladder to Danny Mantussi's and passed the spot where Danny and Tony Golida pretended to sleep.

All the boys knew this was the most difficult part of the plan. The timing had to be just right. They had all hoped this wouldn't be necessary. But the clock plan, the note plan, and the missing shoe plan had not worked. They held their breaths as Ike peered between the bars and reached his hand over the railing. He didn't lean, remembering Mama's warning. Just to be safe, Morton held one of his legs and James Higgins held the other.

"You better throw the water bag, Ike. You better do it already," whispered James.

Ike was known for his good aim. He could hit any noisy cat in the neighborhood. The neighbors were used to the sound of meowing followed by the splat of a bag of water. Ike never threw anything that would hurt the cats, and Mama always said a little water never hurt anyone. A little water wouldn't hurt Arnold and Rosie, either, Ike thought.

Arnold and Rosie were almost to the bottom of the

last ladder when Ike gave the signal. "Now!" he whispered, and the boys sprang into action.

Morton and James Higgins started to meow. Ike took careful aim and dropped the bag of water right on Arnold's head.

Just as they all heard the splat, Danny reached down with his long arm, snatched Arnold's glasses, and handed them to Tony, who handed them up between the iron strips above him to Ike. All the boys smiled or winked or poked one another when they heard the hiss—not of the cats on East 136th Street, but of dripping Arnold.

"Cats," Ike heard Mrs. Mantussi mutter through her opened bedroom window as he clutched Arnold's glasses and dried them on his mattress.

Now the boys were sure they'd stopped Arnold and Rosie. After all, a person who can't see will stop climbing.

And, both dripping wet, Rosie and Arnold did stop.

Arnold sputtered, "Darn, where are my glasses? Funny, I didn't hear them drop."

"*Sh,* my poor wet Arnold. Before you wake Mrs. Mantussi," Rosie warned and soothed at the same time. Then she chuckled softly and whispered, "Ikey must think we're cats."

But then Rosie and Arnold continued down the last ladder as if nothing had happened! Morton scratched his head and James Higgins said, "Huh?" And Ikey knew he must do something with WORDS!

Now came the hardest part of all. Ike had to get Arnold and Rosie not just to stop, but to listen to reason. If he failed, there would be no block wedding. He cracked his knuckles, peeked over the rail, and said, "*PSST, psst,* up here."

Rosie and Arnold stopped and looked up.

Ike cupped one hand over his mouth and in a low voice called, "Arnold, I've got your glasses." Ike waved the glasses. He crossed his fingers and waited for the answer.

An angry, red-faced, dripping Arnold slowly climbed back to Danny Mantussi's fire escape. Ike had to think of something to say—something that would stop the elopement for sure. He had to take a chance.

"You can't elope," Ike called louder than he meant to. But it was so important! "You can't elope," Ike called desperately.

"Ikey," Mama called through the open bedroom window. "What are you screaming in the middle of the night yet? Shush. You sound like the fruitman. A *canteloupe* you call whomsoever? Cursing yet?"

"But Mama," he called back.

"You don't *but mama* ME, you hear?" And in a louder voice she said, "Good night means good night!"

"*Psst,*" Ike called again to Rosie and Arnold. "C'mere. Please don't elope." They both clambered up the ladder to shush him.

Should he spoil the surprise? Ike thought. What would he say when they reached his fire escape? But if Rosie and her boyfriend eloped, ran off to get married, there would be no surprise, altogether. Ike, too, needed some help from God. He looked up a minute, then whispered.

"A surprise wedding is planned, a block wedding. Everyone has worked so hard. You can't spoil everything." There, he'd told. So what else could he have done?

The two huddled together looking up at Ike. "But so much money it must have cost?" whispered Rosie.

"On this block"—Ike spoke more softly than ever—"there is now a special plan for weddings that cost almost nothing. On East One Hundred and Thirty-sixth Street in the Bronx we have the 'handful plan.' "

"The what?" asked Rosie as she climbed back up with Arnold and sat down close to Ike, Morton, and James on the mattress.

"I don't understand," said her boyfriend, sitting down next to her, tightly gripping the metal railing of the fire escape. There was barely enough room for him.

"A high-school graduate is supposed to be smart," Ike whispered to Arnold. "You can't even figure out a handful plan?"

Arnold couldn't even get a word in as Ike continued. "You learn in high school how to break hearts?" Ike said, sounding very much like Mama.

"What?" said Arnold and he leaned over Rosie to get closer to Ike.

"If you elope, there will be broken hearts on East One Hundred and Thirty-sixth Street," Ike explained. "Many broken hearts," he added. "So, you won't elope. You won't spoil the surprise. Right, Rosie? And toi, toi, toi." Ike spit three times over his shoulder in case of evil spirits, and to make extra sure he knocked on the wooden windowsill three times, too, like he was sure Mama would have done.

"You shouldn't even see each other till the wedding," Ike said, "and you just can't elope! Right, Rosie? I hope you won't."

This time he gave Rosie a chance to answer as he watched the moon disappear behind a cloud.

"No," Rosie said, and she patted Ike on the head.

"We won't, Ikey. Thanks," she said and then she looked at Morton.

"I won't tell," Morton whispered, "and your shoes are in the oven."

As Arnold put on the glasses Ike handed him, he whispered to Morton, "Elope has an 'e' on the end." Then, still dripping slightly, he kissed Rosie and climbed down to the street. Sammy, of course, made the kissing noise on his hand. Stopping now and then to wave, Rosie climbed up the fire-escape ladder to her apartment.

Ike was smiling with satisfaction and shaking hands with Morton and James when he realized Mama was in the kitchen now.

"What is going on? What?" she asked, clutching her faded plaid flannel robe, her hair hanging down her back in a dark braid. "And who did you call a canteloupe?" she added.

Ike said, "I didn't call anyone a canteloupe. I said 'I hope, I hope.' I was hoping."

"Hoping?" called Mama.

"Sort of like praying," Ike added, looking up.

"Anything that is like praying is acceptable," said Mama. "Now go to sleep soon, Ikey. Tomorrow will be a busy day."

Ike decided to listen to Mama. As he settled down

under the night sky, Ike hoped that God would listen to Mama, too, and help with the wedding, because he thought he felt a drop of rain!

8. The Block Wedding

Ike woke up early Sunday morning. The rain had turned from a slight drizzle to a downpour. Suddenly both Ike and East 136th Street were soaked. Raindrops bounced off the striped awning on the corner candy store. An automobile stopped and a man got out. He rubbed half an onion on the windshield so the raindrops wouldn't roll on that spot. Ike stared. The Uncle Sam on the tattered billboard looked as if tears were rolling down his cheeks.

Everyone was upset: Ike, Papa, Bessie, Rosie, Morton, Mrs. Weinstein, and Mr. Weinstein—everyone was upset, except Mama. Mama was bustling about decorating the food. She put candy pearls on the wedding cake and a radish cut like a rose on the egg salad.

"Mama," Ike said, "don't you see what's happening outside?"

"I see, I see," said Mama without looking up. Mama refused to get upset.

Bessie started to cry.

"More drops we don't need," Papa said, pointing out the window but talking to Bessie.

"Everybody gets to do a something at Rosie's wedding, and I only get to stay out of the way." Bessie continued sobbing.

Mama patted Bessie's shoulder, then placed another candy pearl on the cake.

Papa moved the candy pearl and added two more to the cake. "Mama, this way would be better still," said Papa. "But what am I decorating? There will be no wedding with this rain. So stop crying, Bessie. Everybody is doing a special something for nothing."

Mama moved the pearl back and added flowers made of pink icing.

"Mama, what are you putting? Flowers there?" Papa said.

"Oy, Papa." Mama put her hand on each side of her head. "A headache I'm getting from your nudging. And Bessie, from putting this flower on the cake I remember my idea from last night, a special something for Bessie to do."

Papa shrugged his shoulders. "It's RAINING." Papa sang the last word.

"What's the special something? Tell me," Bessie begged, tugging on Mama's checked apron and turning off the tears like a faucet.

"If only the rain could stop like Bessie's tears," said Mrs. Weinstein, staring out the window.

"What can Bessie do?" asked Ike, still upset by the rain and more upset by the fact that Mama didn't even seem to notice that the day was spoiled.

Mama stroked Bessie's long hair as she explained. "I saw in a picture in a magazine, a wedding, must have been from the Grand Concourse. And in it was a little girl. She had a job of importance. She dressed in her best dress."

"What did she do, Mama?" asked Bessie.

"She walked slowly, on tiptoe even, and from a basket dropped petals from pink roses so the bride should follow and maybe have a rosy life—who knows? But slowly she walked, Bessie, not like running after a rubber-band ball. So maybe Papa, you could please take Bessie by the hand and get from someone's garden rose petals, a basketful?"

"In the rain?" Papa asked.

Ike thought Mama would say "What rain?" She didn't seem to pay attention to it. But all she said was, "In the rain."

"You can manage here without me?" said Papa.

72

"I will try," said Mama, and breathed a sigh of relief as Papa and Bessie went downstairs.

Finally Ike could stand it no more. "It's raining hard, Mama, rain! R-A-I-N!" He even spelled it. "Don't you see what's happening outside?" Sammy and Dave came into the kitchen. Water dripped from their hair.

"I see, Ikey, I see it. But! I understand," said Mama.

"I don't," answered Ike.

"I don't either," added Morton Weinstein.

"I am in charge of the food for Rosie's wedding," said Mama. "And God is taking care of the cleaning. So if He wants East One Hundred and Thirty-sixth Street to be sparkling clean, who am I to be upset?"

And sure enough: At three o'clock a handful of sunshine came out and so did all the neighbors. By three-thirty the street was blocked with horses from the fire station, and Sammy and Dave had tables lined up along the sidewalk. Patrick, Danny Mantussi, and Tony Golida hung streamers from the trees and made stripes on the gas lamps like barbershop poles.

Guests started arriving. Arnold's father said, "What a good idea. Of course a wedding hall would have been too hot. Outside, with this beautiful breeze here, it is perfect!"

The rabbi arrived at four o'clock and took out four

poles and a fringed prayer shawl of fine white linen to be used as a wedding canopy. And Rosie, acting surprised and delighted, sent Morton out with a job of importance: to choose who would hold up the poles of the chuppah. Ike was asked to hold one pole. He was glad not to have to choose jobs. Dave and Sammy held two more, and the fourth pole Morton handed to tall Danny Mantussi, even though he wasn't Jewish, because, as Morton explained, Danny was big enough to represent the entire block.

At four-fifteen Herbie Friedman's older brothers, the neighborhood musicians, who'd completed five violin lessons, screeched out some wedding music. Morton escorted Arnold's sister, Shirley, down the block to where the crowd had gathered. Ike couldn't help laughing because with Morton's bowed legs and Shirley's knock knees, together they spelled the word "OX." When Morton tripped once trying to avoid a puddle, Patrick giggled and James Higgins said, "Shush!"

Then at four-twenty Bessie, very serious after all her warnings from Mama, walked slowly, inch by inch, down East 136th Street, dropping rose petals one at a time.

At four-thirty Bessie was still walking.

"Hurry up, Bessie," called the uncles.

"A little faster, Bessie darling," called the neighbors.

But Bessie listened to Mama—she walked slowly until her basket of rose petals was empty.

At four thirty-five the groom, Arnold, the high-school graduate, walked down the street with his parents.

Then finally at four-forty the violins played "Here Comes the Bride," and beautiful Rosie in the satin-and-lace dress Mama had made—the East 136th Street business investment—walked down the block. Her arms were hooked onto her father's and her mother's and she tried to keep pace with the music. Mrs. Weinstein walked and wiped her eyes at the same time. Morton was right. Rosie, too, cried all the way to the chuppah.

The rabbi gave the blessing for the wine, and Rosie and Arnold sipped two times from the same cup. Ike swallowed, too, imagining the heavy sweet taste. The rabbi said a lot of things in Hebrew that Ike did not understand. And three people sneezed and one man coughed. When Arnold slipped a ring on Rosie's finger, Ike knew they were almost married.

Then came the moment all had waited for. Arnold lifted his foot high, and CRASH and CRACK he stamped on a fragile wine glass wrapped in cloth. The sound reminded Ike of the broken elephant. But Ike knew this breaking of glass was because in a time of happiness something like the destruction of the ancient Jerusalem Temple must be remembered. Maybe because it makes the happy moment even happier, Ike thought. Well! With the sound of the breaking glass Arnold kissed Rosie and everyone shouted "MAZEL TOV, good luck." Even Mrs. Mantussi, the Golidas, and Mr. and Mrs. Higgins. Sammy made the kissing noise on his hand.

Then four men held Rosie up high on a chair and four more did the same with Arnold and the women danced seven times around Rosie and the men danced seven times around Arnold. Then, since Mama was not a member of the family, something unusual was done. Mr. Weinstein placed Mama on a chair and four more men lifted her high in the air. And the women, led by Mrs. Weinstein, danced a thank-you around her. All the boys clapped to the music. Mama held on to the chair tightly and screamed "Oy!"

Morton leaned over and whispered to Ike, "You should be up on a chair, because without your fire-escape plan there would be no wedding." Ike put his finger to his lips shushing Morton. But he couldn't help swelling with pride when Rosie winked at him from high up on the chair.

76

Then Papa served the wine, and the boys helped bring the salads and sliced challah and potatonik out to the table. Mama sent Ike upstairs to get the sliced herring from the icebox. It had been kept separately so it wouldn't smell up everything. Ike dashed upstairs, grabbed the herring dish, and raced out the apartment door, not realizing one slice of herring had dropped onto the parlor rug. He ran out so fast that he didn't stop to close the door tightly.

When Ike got back to the wedding celebration Mama fixed a plate of herring, challah, egg salad, and potatonik for the rabbi. Of course she put it on her special glass plate. And the rabbi did eat from it proudly.

Then at five-thirty when everyone on East 136th Street and their guests had had something to eat, Mama and Mrs. Weinstein carried out the beautifully decorated, three-tiered, perfect flower-and-pearl wedding cake. All the boys watched Mama except for Danny Mantussi, who fixed a streamer that had come loose from the tablecloth. Mama put the cake down in front of Rosie and Arnold and got everyone's attention with a wave of her hands. "Quiet, everyone." Mama spoke softly, but everyone listened.

"A gift for Rosie and Arnold," Mama announced. "A gift from the whole block."

"A cake is a gift?" one of the groom's relatives muttered. "What kind of gift is that?"

Mama smiled. "Our gift is a cake but it is also a blessing," Mama said. She cleared her throat and stood up tall as she could, being only four feet seven inches in height. "We wish for you, Rosie and Arnold, that your married life should be like this wedding cake. A sweet life . . . made from sharing." And Mama pinched Rosie's cheek until it was red.

Then Mama stepped back and everyone on East 136th Street clapped. Rosie kissed Mama as well as her own mama, papa, and brother. Morton wiped the spot. Then Ike blushed as Rosie kissed him on the cheek, and Sammy made a wolf whistle.

Mama gave Rosie the knife, and with Arnold's hand on hers, Rosie cut the cake. Ike and the boys ate . . . and ate . . . and ate. It was the best cake, ever.

After all the thank-you's and the dancing were done, and all the cake was eaten, the Mantussis and the Golidas threw pennies for the children to pick up. The boys scrambled to get them. "It wishes Rosie and Arnold wealth," explained Danny.

Rice, confetti, and raisins showered down upon the bride and groom as they were sent off in a relative's automobile. The sound of dragging tin cans surprised everyone but Morton and James Higgins. No one knew where Rosie and Arnold were going on their honeymoon, but with the boys' handiwork everyone would know they were "just married."

Mr. Weinstein waved and waved, but Mrs. Weinstein sat down on the curb and cried. Mama walked toward the table, her hands on her heart. Ike followed Mama when she called to him.

Ike looked up at the sky and wondered if he'd drunk too much wine. He saw a smile on the round full moon. So, he thought, God, too, gave a handful to the block wedding on East 136th Street—a handful of sunshine, moonlight, and stars. And Ike was still glancing at that smiling moon, wondering if maybe God, too, had sipped too much leftover Passover wine, when Mama handed Ike her special plate, the plate the rabbi had eaten from, proudly.

"You will please carry this plate upstairs," she said, "and put it in the sink." Mama led the way, her arms filled with tablecloths.

And Ike followed. Although he trembled, remembering the broken glass elephant, he listened to Mama and took the plate. He did not drop the special plate on the outside stoop. And he did not drop the special plate on the inside stairs. But he almost dropped it in the parlor when he heard Mama gasp. The faded parlor rug was crowded—not with an army of boys, but with an army of cats! Gray, black, striped, and blond, they were all licking at the spot where the herring had dropped.

But Ike still did not drop the special plate. He carefully put it in the sink. Then he said, "Scat" to the big striped cat with the crooked tail who hissed at him from Papa's soft parlor chair with the rip.

"Oy!" said Mama. First she raised an eyebrow and said, "You see? You must close the door, Ikey, cats come up!" Then Mama chuckled and added, "So, now we know that no one was left out of this block wedding. Even the cats of East One Hundred and Thirty-sixth Street in the Bronx had a something to eat at Rosie's wedding."

Ike laughed, too. And from the doorway, Papa and Bessie looked surprised as cats scurried past Mama, around either side of Papa's long legs and through the middle, yet!

About the Author

CAROL SNYDER was born and raised in Brooklyn and attended Brooklyn College. In addition to writing, she teaches children with learning disabilities. Mrs. Snyder lives with her husband, a consulting engineer, and their two children in New Jersey, where the family enjoys community volunteer work, painting, photography, and camping trips.

Ike and Mama and the Block Wedding is Mrs. Snyder's second book for children and follows *Ike and Mama and the Once-a-Year Suit,* also published by Coward, McCann & Geoghegan.

About the Artist

A native of New Jersey, CHARLES ROBINSON attended Harvard College and the University of Virginia Law School. After practicing law for a number of years, he decided to devote himself full time to his art. He has illustrated over sixty books, including *The Terrible Wave* by Marden Dahlstedt and Carol Snyder's *Ike and Mama and the Once-a-Year Suit,* and he has won the Gold Medal of the Society of Illustrators. Mr. Robinson, his wife Cynthia, and their three children live in New Vernon, New Jersey.

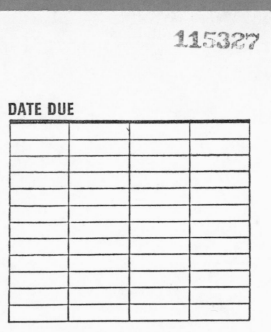
Ohio Dominican College Library

1216 Sunbury Road

Columbus, Ohio 43219

DEMCO